Heinrich N. Ehrenthal

The English Novelists

Heinrich N. Ehrenthal

The English Novelists

ISBN/EAN: 9783337349288

Printed in Europe, USA, Canada, Australia, Japan

Cover: Foto ©Andreas Hilbeck / pixelio.de

More available books at **www.hansebooks.com**

THE

ENGLISH NOVELISTS.

INAUGURAL DISSERTATION

FOR THE ATTAINMENT OF THE DEGREES

OF

DOCTOR OF PHILOSOPHY AND MASTER OF ARTS

AT THE

UNIVERSITY OF \ROSTOCK

BY

HEINRICH NICOLAUS EHRENTHAL

LICENCIATE OF THE COLLEGE OF PRECEPTORS, LOND.

ROSTOCK: ADLER'S ERBEN.

1874.

Preface.

The following is a short review of the History of the English Novel from the time of Richardson and Fielding down to our present days, thus comprising a period of one hundred and thirty years. This essay will be, I am bold to say, a safe guide for the student of the English novel-literature to choose from among the English novels those which are worth reading. The works I have made use of in writing this History of the English Novel are: Chambers' Cyclopaedia of English Literature, History of English Literature by Smith, id. by Spalding, id. by Angus, id. by Craik, The last hundred years of English Literature by Grant, Allibone's Dictionary of English Literature and British and American Authors. Special works on the English Novelists have been written by David Masson: British Novelists and their styles, and by Jeaffreson:

Novels and Novelists. I still wish to remark that the writer who first gave me a taste of English reading was Sir Walter Scott who, undoubtedly, keeps the same high place in the literature of the historical novel as Homer, Thucydides, Demosthenes, Horace, Shakespeare, and Molière in their respective departments of literature.

Contents.

                                                                    Page
Chronological Table of the English Novelists VI

Introduction.
    1. Origin of the modern novel in the literature of Europe . . . 1
    2. Definition and classification of novels 2

Part First. The English Novelists of the eighteenth century.
    Chapter I.
    1. John Bunyan, Defoe, Swift — 2. Richardson, Fielding, Smollett —
    3. Sterne, Goldsmith 3
    Chapter II.
    Romance-writers: Walpole, Reeve, Radcliffe, Lewis, Maturin, Shelley 15
    Chapter III.
    1. Burney, 2. Sophia and Harriet Lee, 3. Godwin 19

Part Second. The English Novelists of the present century.
    Chapter IV.
    Edgeworth, Austen 22
    Chapter V.
    Sir Walter Scott and his imitators 28
    Chapter VI.
    Bulwer Lytton, Dickens, Thackeray 33
    Chapter VII.
    1. Morier — 2. Marryat 42
    Chapter VIII.
    Disraeli, Trollope, Kingsley, Collins 43
    Chapter IX.
    Charlotte Bronte, George Eliot 44

Conclusion.
    1. Statistics of the English Novel 46
    2. Superiority of the English Novel over that of other countries 46
    3. On the Reading of Novels 47

Chronological Table

of

the English Novelists.

Names of the novelists	Dates of their birth & death.	Principal Works	Dates of their publication
John Bunyan	1628—1688	The Pilgrim's Progress	about 1670
Daniel Defoe	1661—1731	Robinson Crusoë	1719
Jonathan Swift	1667—1745	Gulliver's Travels .	1726
Samel Richardson	1689—1761	Pamela	1740 & 1741
Henry Fielding	1707—1754	Tom Jones	1749
Tobias George Smollett	1721—1771	Roderick Random	1748
Lawrence Sterne	1713—1768	Tristram Shandy	1759—1767
Oliver Goldsmith	1728—1774	Vicar of Wakefield	(1764) 1766
Horace Walpole	1717—1797	Castle of Otranto	1764
Miss Clara Reeve	1725—1803	Old English Baron	1777
Mrs. Ann Radcliffe	1764—1823	Mysteries of Udolpho	1794
George Lewis	1775—1818	(The Monk)	1795
Robert Maturin	1782—1824	(Melmoth)	1820
Mrs. Shelley .	1798—1851	(Frankenstein)	1816
Frances Burney	1752—1840	(Evelina)	1778
Sophia Lee ⎰	1750—1824	The Canterbury Tales	1797
Harriet Lee ⎱	1766—1851		
William Godwin	1756—1836	Caleb Williams	1794
Miss Maria Edgeworth	1765—1849	Early Lessons, Popular Tales, Moral Tales, Fashionable Tales	1822—25. 1804, 1809
Miss Jane Austen	1775—1817	Pride and Prejudice	about 1810
Sir Walter Scott	1771—1832	Waverley, Series of Waverley Novels	1814—1831
George Payne Rainsford James	1801—1860	(Richelieu)	1828
William Harrison Ainsworth	1805- living	(The Tower of London)	1840
Sir Edward Bulwer Lytton	1805—1873	Devereux, The last Days of Pompeii, Rienzi &c.	1829, 32, 35
Charles Dickens	1812—1870	Pickwick Papers, Nicholas Nickleby &c.	1837, 39
William Makepeace Thackeray	1811—1863	Vanity Fair, Pendennis, Newcomes	1847, 1850 1853—1855
Benjamin Disraeli	1805- living	(Contarini Fleming)	1830
Anthony Trollope	1815- living	(Doctor Thorne)	1858
Charles Kingsley	1819- living	Westward Ho!	1855
Wilkie Collins	1824- living	The Woman in White, Man and Wife	1850—60, 1870
James Morier	1780—1849.	Hajji Baba	1824
Captain Frederick Marryat	1792—1848	The Naval Officer, Peter Simple	1829, 1832
Charlotte Brontë	1816—1855	Jane Eyre	1848
George Eliot	1820 ?	Adam Bede	1850

Remark. Those works which are put in brackets do not mark a progress in the literature of the novel, neither do they represent a peculiar kind of novels.

Introduction.

1. The literary productions of almost every nation appear at first in poetic form. Among the ancient Greeks Homer sings the great deeds and exploits of the Grecian and Trojan heroes, before Herodotus relates the history of the Persian wars in prosaic language. In the middle age when the spirit of chivalry reigned over Europe the nations celebrated in poetical language either the heroes of antiquity as Alexander the Great or those of the middle age as Charlemagne and his paladines, King Arthur and the knights of the Round Table. After the downfall of chivalry those poetic romances underwent a change in form, and they were written in prosaic language and style. In the XVIIth century these prosaic romances again gave rise in France to a kind of prose literature, the so-called heroic romances[1]), which took their characters chiefly from the ancients, as Horatius Cocles, Mutius Scaevola, Clelia, Cyrus, but invested them with the manners and customs of the time of Louis XIV. The most celebrated authoress in that branch of literature is Mademoiselle de Scudéri who wrote *Grand Cyrus* which contains ten large volumes, *Clelia,* likewise a most voluminous work. This latter contains the siege of Rome by Porsenna. All those events known from history are related in it; but the chief agent of the whole story is not Roman bravery and patriotism, but love. One scarcely can open the book without meeting love-scenes.

These romances were translated into English, e. g. *Clelia translated into English 1656,* and were imitated after the restoration of Charles II, e. g. *The Obliging Mistress or the fashionable Gallant.*

---

[1]) cf. Chambers's Cyclopaedia I. 773.

1

A Novel by a Person of Quality. London 1678. They were read in the highest circles of society and were even recommended by the clergy. However, they could not escape of being ridiculed, and this was done most successfully by Scarron in his *Roman Comique* which contains a series of stories in which the customary way of representing the heroes as paragons of lovers is persifflated. To Cervantes, the author of *Don Quixote,* and Le Sage, the author of *the Adventures of Gil Blas* the honour is due to have given more useful purposes to those prosaic fictions by pointing out the foibles and follies of ordinary life and describing the customs and manners of their time [2]). These authors exercised great influence on the department of novel literature at its first appearance in England.

2. Before, however, entering on the history of the origin and the development of the English novel let us define and subdivide the romances and the novels; both are prose fictions: the romances have for their object wondrous and miraculous events, whereas the novels represent real life [3]). — In the following pages I propose to speak of both kinds of prose fiction.

The various kinds of novels may be subdivided into the following divisions [4]):

I. Historical novels which relate epochs of past or recent history; the personages are either real or so invented as to agree with the general character of the time.

II. Descriptive novels picturing the aspect and customs of near or distant countries. As subdivisions I may mention the marine and military novels; the former relating scenes at sea, the latter describing the horrors and cruelties of war.

III. Common novels, i. e. tales of social life. In those novels life is represented as it is, and not as it ought to be. Every day's talk and doing, man's passions and feelings are described.

IV. Moral novels, i. e. tales written with the object of imparting some moral truth.

---

[2]) cf. Smollet's Preface to Roderick Random.

[3]) Scott describes a Romance as "a fictious narrative in prose or verse, the interest of which turns upon marvellous and uncommon incidents;" being thus opposed to the kindred term Novel which the same author defines as "a fictious narrative differing from the Romance, because the events are accomodated to the ordinary train of human events, and the modern state of society."

[4]) cf. Smith's Engl. Lit. 480.

Let us now see who were the founders of the English novel and trace its history down to the present day. It is a vast field which opens before our eyes where hundreds of names and thousands of works crowd upon our mind. Let us try to make a good selection of the best names and their best works.

Part First.

Chapter I.

1. **John Bunyan** (1628—1688) is regarded by some as the father of the English novel on account of his work *The Pilgrim's progress from this World to that which is to come*[5]).

However, we may rather consider Bunyan as an allegorist than a novelist; for he represents imaginary ideas, like hope, despair, as acting persons, and does not relate incidents of common, real life. Others claim **Daniel Defoe** (1661—1731) the author of *Robinson Crusoë* of which the first part was published in 1719, as the founder of the English novel[6]). *Robinson Crusoë*, however, is no real novel; it does not give the description of the life and manners of any time; for the hero is entirely secluded from the human race, and his adventures and troubles which he alone has to undergo on a solitary island, are simply related. *Robinson Crusoë* is a tale of successive adventures. Defoe has given in the plainest language of truth the description of every incident; but he has drawn no characters. In order of time I mention Dean **Swift** (1667—1745), as author of the political romance *Gulliver's Travels* published in 1726, whose first part, a voyage to Lilliput, is a satire on the English politics and statesmen in especial and the other three parts, a voyage to Brobdingnag, a voyage to Laputa, a voyage to the Houyhnhms, are a satire on the whole human

---

[5]) cf. Hallam's Intr. to the Lit. of Eur. IV 331. "John Bunyan may pass for the father of our novelists."

[6]) cf. Smith's Engl. Lit. ch. XVII 2: "The founder of the English Novel is Daniel Defoe."

race. Never was there found a more biting sarcasm as expressed
in the comparison of the Yahoos with mankind. After those few
words about the great English satirist let us return to our question
who was the founder of the modern English novel.

2. If neither John Bunyan, nor Daniel Defoe may be said
to have originated the English novel, this honour is undoubtedly
due to Samuel Richardson [7]), with whom we may mention together
Fielding and Smollett as the three great patriarchs of the English
novel. These men were the first who gave in England a description of the manners and customs of their time, of the feelings
and passions of men, who related the common incidents of life,
its sorrows and joys. From those men therefore who lived in the
middle of the last century, we have to trace the English novel.

Samuel Richardson was born in Derbyshire in 1689. His
father being poor he enjoyed only a very moderate education, but
distinguished himself already at school as a story-teller. Young
Richardson found especially willing listeners among the female sex,
and at the age of thirteen he carried on the love-correspondence
of three young women in humble life [8]). He learned the profession
of printing and, by his industry, he made a considerable fortune
which he husbanded with the greatest economy. He died in the
year 1761 at the age of seventy-two years, much lamented by his
friends for his many good qualities, for he was an honest, upright,
painstaking man, but not without vanity and too much sensibility.
The author's literary career is already foreshadowed in his juvenile
inclinations of telling moral stories and in his great facility of
writing letters. He was no writer by profession; he only wrote
on the request of some of his friends in the year 1739 until 1740
his first novel *Pamela or Virtue Rewarded* which created an
immense sensation [9]); for until that time there were published no
other stories but monstrous and inflated romances according to
the French style, which described in a bombast style the loves
of princes and princesses; but *Pamela* was the first work which
related in simple and natural words events of real life. This
story, like Richardson's other two novels, is written in form of

---

[7]) cf. Smith's Engl. Lit. ch. XVII. 5. and Allibone's Dict. of Authors:
"Samuel Richardson gained the title of The Inventor of the English Novel."

[8]) cf. Richardson's Life and Correspondence I Introd. XXXIX., XL.
(Allibone's Dict. of Authors 1797.)

[9]) cf. Life of Richardson by Sir Walter Scott.

letters: Pamela, the daughter of poor but honest parents, enters the service of a lady who kindly receives her and brings her up as a gentlewoman. On her deathbed the lady recommends the girl to her son who soon feels a violent passion to her. He attempts to seduce her, but she triumphantly resists all his temptations and violences. In her utmost distress, after a fruitless attempt to escape, she will drown herself, and is only held back by the thought of God. Ultimately she is married to her former persecutor whom, notwithstanding all the afflictions he had formerly heaped upon her, she never could hate. The author shows in this novel his accurate knowledge of the human heart: Pamela is a good maiden who, however, accepts too eagerly the hand of her former, villainous persecutor. He himself although described as generous, cannot gain our affection because, slave of his passion, he only consents to marry poor, virtuous Pamela after all other means have failed to possess her. The moral tendency of the book was at the time of its publication much praised: Pope said it would produce more good than twenty volumes of sermons, even clergymen recommended it from the pulpit [10]). We feel perhaps astonished, for there are many obscene passages which the author would have done better to leave out altogether. — I recall the scene where Mr. B. is in disguise of the maid-servant, but we must remember that this novel was written at a time when the licentious habits of the court and the higher circles had blunted their delicate moral feeling, and the reading public did not feel any abhorrence to read such a plain description of vice. In 1749 Richardson published his second novel: *The History of Clarissa Harlowe,* his masterwork [11]). In a separate double correspondence between two young virtuous ladies on the one side, and two licentious gentlemen on the other side, the author treats matters which are of the greatest interest for every family. The question of marriage is much touched upon. He warns young ladies to form alliances with dissolute young men, and parents to force their children into marriage. This novel caused the greatest excitement among the reading-public, and whilst it was in progress of publication, ladies addressed themselves by letter to the author

---

[10]) If all other books were to be burnt "Pamela and the Bible should be preserved." (A critic of Richardson's time: Allibone's Dict. of Authors 1798.)

[11]) cf. Sir Walter Scott's Life of Richardson.

imploring him for the conversion of Lovelace and his union with Clarissa.

Richardson's last novel: *Sir Charles Grandison,* like his predecessors written in a series of letters, published in 1753, was intended to depict a good, righteous, christian gentleman. Thus in *Pamela* Richardson represents virtue persecuted, but finally rewarded, in *Clarissa Harlowe,* virtue persecuted and afflicted in this world, in *Sir Charles Grandison,* virtue without any trials[12]): "Victorious, happy, glorious."

The next great novelist whom I have already mentioned as one of the three founders of the English novel, was **Henry Fielding.** He was born 1707 at Sharpham Park, Sommersetshire, and educated at Eton. Afterwards he went to the university of Leyden to study the law. At the death of his father, General Fielding, he returned to England, and in order to gain a livelihood he embraced the literary profession and wrote several dramatic pieces for the stage which, however, are of no value. His manners were extravagant, and he soon dissipated the fortune which he had got by his marriage. Then he returned to the profession of law, and went on writing dramas. In consequence of the publication of *Pamela* by Richardson, he wrote *Joseph Andrews* intended to ridicule the tone and moral standard of that novel. *Journey from this World to the Next* and *The Life of Jonathan Wild* are his next works, the former full of political allusions — the author was adhering to liberal and anti-jacobite principles — the latter, a very satirical tale. In 1749 he published his completest novel *Tom Jones,* the first and truest description of familiar life. His health being broken down by labour and excesses Fielding was advised to try a warmer climate, and he departed for Lisbon where he died in 1754. In speaking of Fielding's literary productions I shall confine myself to his greatest prosaic fiction *Tom Jones* which is held to be the most accomplished novel[13]). The bill of fare of this novel, as the author himself pleasantly uses that term in the first chapter of the first book, is very rich; it keeps up through the various incidents our anxiety to know the final development. The characters of the wild, ingenuous, not faultless, but upright and

---

[12]) cf. ibidem. Charles Grandison being styled the
"Faultless monster that the world ne'er saw." (Allibone's Dict.)
[13]) cf. Dr. Beatti: "Since the days of Homer the world has not seen a more artful epic fable. (Allibone's Dict. of Authors.)

open hero "who was never backward to help the distressed" but
who was so much debased as to be kept by a lady for some time,
of the soft heroïne, of the good, benevolent squire Allworthy, the
magistrate of the village "who never judges any cause in a fit of
passion," of the rough, robust country gentleman Mr. Western,
are as many copies of real nature. The minor characters of the
theologian and pedagogue Thwackum and of the philosopher
Square, of the smooth and somewhat hypocritical young Master
Blifil are equally well drawn. The character of Lady Bellaston
shows the deep degradation of many a lady of high fashion of
that time who only gratified their natural appetite without any
sense of decency. The story of the family of Mrs. Miller, her
daughter Miss Nancy, and Mr. Nightingale shows the author's
deep intuition into the human heart and its feelings. Mr. Nightingale
makes love to Miss Nancy without the honourable intention of
marrying her, breaks his promise of marriage when the girl is
undone and causes great misfortunes to that poor but honest
family. The author of all this mischief pities the poor victim,
till at last by the influence of our hero he marries the deceived
girl. The chapter describing the scene at the play-house in which
Fielding immortalises his friend Garrick, still calls our attention:
Partridge, the companion of our hero Tom Jones, had gone to
the play and being told that Garrick who had represented Hamlet,
was the best player, exclaimed: "He the best player! Why I
could act as well as he myself. I am sure if I had seen a ghost,
I should have looked in the very same manner, and done just as
he did." Truly no better eulogy could have been paid to Garrick's
genius than this criticism. Referring to the moral tone of *Tom
Jones* I cannot agree with the author who says that his reader
"will find in the whole course of his work nothing prejudicial to
the cause of religion and virtue, nothing inconsistent with the
strictest rule of decency, nor which can offend even the chastest
eye in the perusal"[14]). He often introduces scenes of too low a
character, however, it is true that he recommends "goodness and
innocence."

In imitation of Homer, "the prose Homer of human nature"
— this name has been given to Fielding by Byron — intersperses
many similes throughout his work as the comparison of the screa-

---

[14]) vide Dedicatory epistle prefixed to Tom Jones.

ming Sommersetshire mob with a herd of cows, or the comparison of two pigeons overtaken by thunderstorm in the wood with the lovers Sophia Western and Tom Jones when Mr. Western came swearing destruction to Tom Jones. I still remark that Fielding also takes. many a simile from the English national sport of hunting, e. g. "there arrived a noise not unlike in loudness to that of a pack of hounds let out from their kennel".

The digression of the *Man of the Hill* [15]) is tedious for the reader and without any connexion with the whole story of the book; it is a tale included in another tale, and the reader will be too easily induced to leave it out in order to get on with the course of the story; the same may be said of the incident of Captain Waters' lady. The only connexion which may be argued to exist between the history of the *Man of the Hill* and that of our hero, is that the Man of the Hills recalls the time of the Revolution of 1688 when the Stuarts were expelled from England, and the tale refers to the year 1745 when the Stuarts made an attempt to throw over the Hanoverian dynasty and to regain the throne of their ancestors. Thus the Man of the Hill represents the past, and the hero of the story, Tom Jones, the present time of the writer.

The interest which the student of novel-writing must feel for *Tom Jones,* is still heightened by the introductory chapters which the author puts at the beginning of each of the nineteen books into which the whole story is divided. In these introductory chapters Fielding, as the author of a "new province of writing," deposes the rules of novel-writing. The great laws which Fielding lays down for every novelist, are: firstly, "he must keep within the bounds of possibility"; secondly, "he must keep within the rules of probability" thirdly, he must maintain the conversation of character that is to say, "the actions must be such as may not only be within the compass of human agency, and which human agents may probably be supposed to do; but they should be likely for the very actors and characters themselves to have performed; "for what may be only wonderful and surprising in one man, may become improbable, or indeed impossible, when related of another" [16]).

---

[15]) vide Tom Jones VIII. ch. XI—XV.
[16]) cf. Tom Jones by Fielding Book VIII. ch. I.

The introductory chapter of the ninth book speaks of the qualification of novelists: The business of a novel-writer is to invent a good story and to tell it well. Now, in no other department of literature there will be so many who attempt to write, without any qualification and learning, as in the department of novel-writing; because to write on sciences and arts or critical essays there is required "some little degree of learning and knowledge", whereas, to the composition of novels, nothing is necessary, as many seem to think, "but paper, pen, and ink with the manual capacity of using them"[17]). But a real novelist must possess genius, i. e. invention and judgement; then he must possess learning and a good knowledge of the history of the belles-lettres; besides he must have a good insight into the characters and customs of men through conversation with men of all ranks in society as well of the high as of the low classes. Lastly the writer must have sympathy with his subject; for what the author himself does not feel, never the reader will feel. Thus Fielding puts down, in a very minute way, the laws of writing novels and the necessary qualification of a novelist; we, therefore, must consider Fielding not as a mere story-teller, but as a critical, literary man. Before dismissing Fielding I still refer to that most poetically written invocation in the first chapter of the thirteenth book of Tom Jones, in which the author invokes Genius, Humanity, Learning and Experience, and expresses his hope of immortality. And let us add that Fielding's immortality reposes on his *Tom Jones* [18]) which Gibbon describes as "the first of ancient or modern romances" and La Harpe, as "le premier roman du monde et le livre le mieux fait de l'Angleterre."

The third great novelist is **Tobias George Smollett,** born 1721 in Scotland. He descended from a noble family, was educated at Dunbarton, went to Glasgow to embrace the medical profession and was apprenticed to a surgeon at Glasgow. After the death of his grandfather he repaired to London to try his fortune as a surgeon either in the navy or the army. Having got a situation as a surgeon-mate in the navy he sailed to the West-Indies where he took part at the unfortunate expedition of Carthagena which he afterwards described in his novel *Roderick Random.* After his

---

[17]) vide Tom Jones by Fielding. IX. ch. 1.
[18]) cf. Gibbon (Allibone's dict. of authors sub Fielding 593).

return to London he made several attempts to gain a livelihood by literary productions, however with little or no success. In the year 1748, when Fielding's master-work *Tom Jones* had not yet appeared, he published his first novel *Roderick Random* which met with great success. In the year 1751 he published *Peregrine Pickle* and 1753 *The Adventures of Ferdinand Count Fathom.* Two years later he brought out a translation of *Don Quixote* and wrote himself a novel in the manner of this Spanish novel: *The Adventures of Sir Launcelot Greaves* which, however, cannot bear a comparison with the Spanish original. Besides these novels Smollett wrote many critics and a *History of England.* In 1770 he set out for Italy in order to restore his health and resided at Leghorn where he composed his last work *Humphrey Clinker*, written like Richardson's works in a series of letters; it is the most laughable of his novels [19]) though he wrote it whilst broken down by disease being about to make that last step whence no man returns. He died at Leghorn in 1771. Thus the author of *Roderick Random* shared the same fate with the author of *Tom Jones*: Both died and were buried in foreign land.

Let us now say some more words about the author's chief work *Roderick Random* and his general character as a novelist.

The great models which Smollett took in writing his novels, were Cervantes' *Don Quixote* and Le Sage's *Gil Blas*. They were the first novels of Spain and France which represented real life without any supernatural and miraculous agencies. The law of possibility on which Fielding afterwards insists in his *Tom Jones* is likewise put up by Smollett, and it may be said to have been observed throughout the manifold adventures which happened to the hero. The law of probability may be said to have been violated in several instances, as in the hero's meeting his father Don Rodrigo and in the adventures of Thompson. The vicissitudes through which the hero passes, are the most variegated. He was at first apprenticed to an apothecary and entered the medical service in the navy where he had to suffer many hardships from the captain and the ship's doctor. On his return to England he became valet-de-chambre to a lady and got enamoured of her niece Narcissa.

---

[19]) "The novel of Humphrey Clinker is, I do think, the most laughable story that has ever been written since the goodly art of novel-writing began." W. M. Thackeray: Engl. Aumourists. (Allibone's Dict. of Authors.)

On leaving the service he was carried over to France by smugglers, then he enrolled as a soldier in the French army, fought at the battle of Dettingen, returned to England and became a fortune-hunter and gamester. At last he made a succesful voyage to Guinea, Paraguay and Jamaica whence he returned a rich man and finally married Narcissa. The moral tone of the novel is very low indeed from the first chapter to the very last words. Scenes are described with a coarseness of language which offend every decent feeling. In vindication of the author we may say "ridendo castigat mores". The most villain characters are introduced amongst whom are certainly those of Earl Strutwell, a profligate of quite an unnatural vice, and Lord Straddle who, abusing their titles of nobility, strip young men of what fortune they may still have, pretending to procure them some place under government. The hero himself cannot be said to have a high moral standing; he yields up to every bad inclination, violates the duty of gratitude towards his companion Strap whom he only uses as his tool, and squanders away the little money that his friend had earned. And what is the recompense of Strap's single-heartedness? He finally gets married with a former prostitute who, it must be owned, had abandoned her vicious mode of life. Smollett's sea-characters as that of Lieutenant Bowling, whose very speech, even when on land, is tinged with maritime terms, represent the true original English tar, depicted from the author's own experience [20]). The history of Melopoyn, an uncessful author, is included in this novel. It shows the intrigues which the managers of the stage employ by refusing the works of authors.

In Melopoyn's disappointments Smollett depicted what he himself had to suffer when he wished to bring his tragedy *The Regicide* on the stage. I cannot leave Smollett without observing that he was one of those unhappy "Authors by Profession" who work their whole life and perish for want of food. He himself speaks of his disappointments in his literary career in the following manner: "Had some of those who were pleased to call themselves my friends been at any pains to deserve the character, and told me ingenuously what I had to expect in the capacity of an author, when I first professed myself of that venerable fraternity, I should in all probability have spared myself the incredible labour and

---

[20]) vide Roderick Random by Smollet ch. III.

chagrin I have since undergone"[21]). Whilst the public was taking delight at his master-works, and the booksellers were making money from his books, their author lived and died in poverty leaving a widow in solitude and misery. "Yet dead a monumental column was raised on his birthplace!"

3. After having spoken of those three great founders of the English novel, Richardson, the great painter of the human heart, who wrote his works from meditation, Fielding and Smollett who represented actual life and wrote their works from experience — authors who even after a lapse of more than hundred years had no superior[22]), only a few rivals — we shall turn to two authors, dissimilar to each other, of whom the one represented the oddities of human nature, the other depicted quiet, domestic life: Sterne and Goldsmith.

Laurence Sterne was born in Ireland in 1713. He studied divinity at Cambridge and obtained the living of the rectory of Sutton where he lived nearly twenty years.. After having published two unregarded sermons, he went to London 1759 to publish the first two volumes of his most singular novel: *The Life and Opinions of Tristram Shandy*. In the next years he went on publishing the following volumes of the novel till in the year 1767 the ninth and last volume appeared. Meanwhile he had made two tours to the continent, France and Italy, which gave rise to his *Sentimental Journey through France and Italy* which he published in 1768. He died in a miserable lodging having none of his friends or relatious around him[20]) — althoug he was married and had a daughter.

Tristram Shandy does not contain a contiguous story, but it is a string of more or less connected events and episodes of which the same persons whose oddities and quaintnesses the author describes, play the principal parts. It is written with great sarcasm and humour; its morals are rather low. The characters in their odd peculiarity are masterly drawn. Who will ever forget the good, kind, old soldier Uncle Toby with his hobby-horse, the science of fortification, or his simple Corporal Trim! Mr. Shandy is represented as an odd philosopher, a man of great learning —

---

[21]) vide D'Israeli's Miscellanies of Literature.
[22]) cf. Chambers's Cyclopaedia I. Novelists 774.
[20]) cf. Smith's Engl. Lit. XVII. 348.

to him Sterne imputes his vast stock of reading — Widow Wad-
mann is a lusty woman. The minor characters are equally well
drawn: Dr. Slop, the quackdoctor, Yorrick, the clergyman and
Mrs. Bridget, the waiting-woman. *Tristram Shandy* made great
noise in the world at its appearence; many attacked it on account
of its low morals. Sterne's private life, although a clergyman,
seems according to the accounts of his contemporaries not to have
been exempt of blame. "He was more dissolute," says Garrick,
"in his conduct than in his writings, and generally drove every
female away by his ribaldry. He degenerated in London like an
ill-transplanted shrub; the incense of the great spoiled his head,
and their ragouts his stomach. He grew sickly and proud — an
invalid in body and mind." There is one objection made to Sterne
that he borrowed much from other writers, especially from Rabelais,
and some even call him a plagiarist. Certainly he had made a
vast use of other authors; but we owe him to have brought the
thoughts and ideas of old forgotten writers to our knowledge[24]);
and besides he possessed so much originality of which Uncle Toby
and Corporal Trim are eternal witnesses, that we may not be too
severe upon him for having borrowed some thoughts and sentences
from other writers; certainly he has made a good use of it.
Referring to the author's *Sentimental Journey through France
and Italy* I may call it an "essay on human nature;" there are
plenty of adventures, many of an indelicate character, which all
betray the author as a sentimentalist.

Leaving that humorous writer we come to one of the most
versatile writers of that age: **Oliver Goldsmith** who, as it is
written, on the monument erected to his memory at Westminster-
Abbey "nullum fere scribendi genus non tetigit, nullum quod tetigit,
non ornavit." He was born in Ireland in 1718, his father being a
poor clergyman. His life offers the greatest vicissitudes: at first at
the university of Dublin, then at Edinburgh whither he went to
study medicine, afterwards for many years he travelled as a poor
scholar through Holland, France, Switzerland, Germany and Italy.
In 1756 he returned to England and was alternately employed at
schools as a miserable usher, or as a medical drudge, or writing
for booksellers and periodicals. The publication of the poem *The
Traveller* in the year 1764 earned great fame for him, and two years

---

[24]) cf. Allibone's Dict. of Authors. 2243.

later *The Vicar of Wakefield* appeared. It is on this work that his reputation chiefly rests. He had already written it two years before, but the bookseller did not dare to publish it before the author's name had become known. He wrote two comedies: *The Good Natured Man* and *She stoops to conquer,* the latter of which has maintained its place on the English stage until the present day. After having thus appeared as a poet, a dramatist, and a novelist, the author composed several historical works: *History of Rome, History of England, History of Greece,* and one on natural history: *History of Animated Nature.* He died in 1774, a victim of his medical skill or rather unfitness, refusing every other medical advice.

Oliver Goldsmith was of a kind and generous temper: he was given up to the passion of gambling — at that time as Fielding informs us, the ruling passion of young men — but not from avarice; for he was regardless of money, and was even benevolent to excess. Let us now consider Goldsmith as a novelist. *The Vicar of Wakefield* gives us a picture of family-life and describes the struggles of that vast class of badly paid curates of the English church who have to live on a small income as gentlemen and to keep a large family. This work excells by the purity of its morals although some parts are not fit to be read by the young; it will always be a master-work of delicate and gentle writing[25]); the plot however, offers many inconsistencies and improbabilities. "The hero" of this novel — I cannot choose better words than those of Goldsmith — "unites in himself the three greatest characters upon earth; — he is a priest, a husbandman, and the father of a family"[26]). His first character is clearly shown from his behaviour at the jail where he tries to bring to repentance even the outcasts of humanity who in the beginning only scoff at him; referring to his second character as a true husband I mention his peculiar tenet of being a monogamist i. e. that he "maintained it as unlawful for a priest of the Church of England, after the death of his wife, to take a second." His true love as a father pervades the whole story: you may take the scene of the fire where he rushes, with peril to his own life, through the flames to save his dear little babes, or when he goes in pursuit of his daughter who had been seduced by her villainous lover, or when he gives

---

[25]) cf. Sir Walter Scott's Life of Goldsmith.
[26]) vide Advertisement to the Vicar of Wakefield by Goldsmith.

his blessing to his eldest son who is going to leave for London
to make his fortune. Mrs. Primrose, the wife of the vicar, is
equally well drawn as a loving mother who is proud of her
children, but is not so quick to forgive her forlorn daughter as
her husband.

The discription of the quiet, happy country-life and the modest,
innocent pleasures at the humble fireside of the vicar are most
pleasing. The two stories of Jenkinson who sold a gross of green,
paltry spectacles to little Moses, Dr. Primrose's son, and who
swindled Dr. Primrose by giving him a valueless draft payable at
sight as payment for a horse, are cleverly told and true to reality.
The generosity, however, is carried too far by giving five hundred
pounds reward to this same rogue who had also been instrumental
in the seduction of Miss Olivia, Dr. Primrose's eldest daughter, —
for an action which he had only done on his own mean interest.
I still remark that from a passage occurring in this book we see
that Defoe's Robinson Crusoë and Fielding's Tom Jones were the
current literature of ladies at that time.

Chapter II.

In this chapter we shall speak of the writers of romances,
at the head of whom we must place Horace Walpole, the author
of the *Castle of Otranto*. Walpole not knowing what succes his
work would meet with and not wishing to expose himself to the
criticism of the day, published *The Castle of Otranto, a Gothic
story,* at first anonymously pretending that the book was found in
the library of an ancient Catholic family in the north of England
and was printed at Naples, in the black letter, in the year 1529.
Most were imposed by the author and believed the book was, old.
When, however, this romance had been favourably received and a
second edition was called forward, Walpole owned the ownership.
A few words will suffice concerning the life of Horace Walpole.
He was born 1717 and was the third son of the Whig minister
Sir Robert Walpole. He studied at Eton and Cambridge where
the poet Gray was one of his schoolfellows, travelled on the Con-
tinent, returned to England and entered the Houses of Parliament.
Meeting with no success in politics he retired from public life to
live secluded in his Gothic Mansion at Strawberry Hill, near

Twickenham. He was a lover of Gothic architecture and antiquities and occupied himself as a dilettante with literature. He died in 1797.

The *Castle of Otranto* introduced quite a new style into English literature. "In the ancient romance all was imagination and improbability; in the modern romance, i. e. novel as Fielding's, nature is always intended to be and sometimes has been copied with success." The author's attempt was to blend these two kinds of romances. The chief agencies of the tale are wondrous and mysterious, passing beyond the limits of real life; though we cannot believe the wondrous events of the story, yet it excites the reader's surprise and terror. I cannot help copying part of a letter written by Mr. Gray to Horace Walpole in the year 1764 to show the effect which the reading of the book may produce: "It engages our attention here (i. e. at Cambridge), makes some of us cry a little, and all, in general, afraid to go to bed o'nights" [27]). On the other side the author reproduces his different characters as real personages acting under the influence of their superstitious belief. In Manfred we recognise the feudal tyrant, in Hippolita his soft, loving, submitting wife, in Mathilda and Isabella gentle, kind girls who are mutually jealous of each other in their love-affairs. The hero of the romance in the young peasant who ventures his life in protecting the safety of "fair damsels."

This romance illustrates the terrible moral lesson that "the sins of the fathers are visited on their children to the third and fourth generation."

"Terror, the author's principal engine, prevents the story from ever languishing; and it is often contrasted by pity, so that the mind is kept up in a constant vicissitude of exciting emotions." Horace Walpole had many imitators amongst whom I mention Miss Clara Reeve and Mrs. Radcliffe. **Miss Clara Reeve,** the daughter of a clergyman, one of a family of eight children, was born in 1725 at Ipswich. In 1777 she published *A Champion of Virtue, a Gothic story* whose title she afterwards changed into that of the *Old English Baron.* She herself calls this romance "a literary offspring [26]) of the *Castle of Otranto,* written upon the

---

[27]) vido Novelists' Library, London; Preface written by Walter Scott to Walpole's Castle of Otranto.

[26]) vide Preface of the Old English Baron by Miss Clara Reeve.

same plan, with a design to unite the most attractive and interesting circumstances of the ancient Romance and modern Novel." It differs from Walpole's romance in so far as the authoress made a more limited use of the wondrous and miraculous agencies; she tries to keep the story within the bounds of probability. She has written some more romances which, as Walter Scott says, "are all marked by excellent good sense, pure morality, and a competent command of those qualities which constitute a good romance" [29]). She died at her native town at the age of seventy-eight years in 1803.

Miss Clara Reeve was followed by a still greater writer: **Mrs. Ann Radcliffe.** She was born in London 1764 where she died 1823. She is the founder of a new school of prose fiction of which the chief agent is terror in its wildest fancy. Her best renowned romances are: *The Romance of the Forest,* 1791, *The Mysteries of Udolpho,* 1794, and *The Italian,* 1797. The authoress, great force consists in describing scenes of horror and sinfulness. Her tales are terrible and dreadful. Even in depicting landscapes of which she has a great power, she introduces gloomy pictures of scenery. The gifted authoress knows how to arouse our curiosity, even keen suspense mingled with terror in the course of her tales. Her descriptions of pathetic scenes are masterly, such as the introduction of *The Mysteries of Udolpho* which relates the death of Madame St. Aubert and her husband. The last words of M. St. Aubert when on his death-bed, which he spoke to his poor, forlorn daughter Emily, are a true picture of the tenderest paternal feelings and cares. The love between Valancourt and Emily which was engendered amidst melancholy circumstances is touchingly narrated. I still refer to one scene in which this authoress, like many an author since the time of Homer, has depicted the fidelity and attachement of the dog to its master. I quote the following passage which, I think, may rival with any description ever given of "man's faithful companion." I premiss a few words to its explanation. St. Aubert who had been travelling with his daughter Emily had died on the journey. She, therefore, returned alone home. She had just arrived at the gate of the chateau when Theresa, the old housekeeper, came to welcome her. "Manchon

---

[29]) vide Novelist's Library, London. Preface written by Walter Scott to Miss Clara Reeve's Old English Baron.

also came running and barking; and when his young mistress alighted, fawned, and played round her, gasping with joy. — The dog still fawned and ran round her, and then flew towards the carriage with a short quick bark. Ah, ma'amselle! My poor master! said Theresa, Manchon's gone to look for him. Emily sobbed aloud; and on looking towards the carriage, which still stood with the door open, saw the animal spring into it, and instantly leap out, and then with his nose on the ground, run towards the horses. — The dog now came running to Emily, then returned to the carriage, and then back again to her, whining and discontented. Poor rogue! said Theresa, thou hast lost thy master — thou may'st well cry [30]!" The gists of the story of *The Romance of the Forest* and *The Mysteries of Udolpho* are the same: two lovers are separated from each other by their tyrannical, selfish and unjust guardians. In both she taught the same moral lesson, "that though the vicious can sometimes pour affliction upon the good, their power is transient and their punishment certain; and that innocence, though oppressed by injustice, shall, supported by patience, finally triumph over misfortune [31]!"

Amongst the numerous followers of Mrs. Radcliffe whom I have already mentioned above as the founder — I may say — of the terrible romantic school of prose fiction, I only refer to **Mathew Gregory Lewis** (1775—1818) who wrote at the age of twenty *The Monk* containing episodes of the wandering Jew [32]), and to **Robert Maturin** (died 1824) whose wildest romance is *Melmoth* in which the hero having made a compact with the devil lives a century and a half and performs the greatest monstrosities [33]).

In connection with the preceding writers of romances I mention Mrs. **Shelley** (1798 -- 1851), daughter of the novelist William Godwin, as authoress of *Frankenstein*. It was written in 1816 whilst the authoress was at Geneva in company with her husband and Lord Byron. Its chief argument runs thus: Frankenstein, a student at university who had occupied himself a long time with the occult sciences, at last succeded to construct a living gigantic being; "it was on a dreary night of November" at one o'clock in the morning that the creature first shewed signs of life. Awful

---

[30]) vide Mysteries of Udolpho by Mrs. Radcliffe.
[31]) vide Conclusion of The Mysteries of Udolpho by Mrs. Radcliffe.
[32]) vide Smith's Engl. Lit. ch. XXIII.
[33]) vide Chamber's Cycl. of Engl. Lit. II. 475.

was that being's countenance!" A mummy endued with animation could not be so hideous as that wretch". The monster being shut out from all mankind urged Frankenstein to make him a helpmate. The student having undertaken the work destroyed it himself when almost done. The demon then committed a series of crimes; he murdered Frankenstein's bride on her wedding-night. Frankenstein perished on the pursuit of his tormentor who, after his maker's death, withdrew to the northern countries to pass his life in solitude. "Frankenstein, says Sir Walter Scott, has passages which appal the mind and make the flesh creep" [34]). Mrs. Shelley has overcome the great difficulty in this story to let appear something impossible as having really taken place.

Chapter III.

Four authors amongst whom there are three ladies, will occupy us in this chapter. They stand in order of time between Richardson, Fielding and Smollett on the one side, and the more modern novelists on the other side, viz. Miss Frances Burney, Miss Sophia and Harriet Lee, and William Godwin.

Miss **Frances Burney** (1752—1840) wrote and got published, without the knowledge of her father, her first novel *Cecilia or a Young Lady's Entrance into the World,* which was followed in 1782 by her second novel *Evelina.* In 1786 Miss Burney got an appointment at the court of Queen Charlotte where she remained till her marriage with a French refugee Comte d'Arblay. After her marriage she wrote a third volume *Camilla.* The authoress paints the fashions of the English society, their oddities and peculiarities. Her heroines are delicate and bashful. There are humorous scenes as the pretended attack of high way-robbers on two ladies with which a love-scene is intermingled [35]). I here wish to remark that in many novels the chief subject which is spoken about is love; for this reason Johnson also defines a novel as "a smooth tale generally of love"; however, in the works of first-rate English novelists love-scenes occur only occasionally, and other important social and moral questions are treated.

---

[34]) vide Scott: Lon. Quart. Rev., May 1818, 379—385. (Allibone's Dict.)
[35]) vide Evelina by Burney, Chambers's Cycl. II. 145.

Sophia Lee (1750—1824) and **Harriet Lee** (1766—1851) known as the authoresses of the Canterbury Tales, a series of romantic fictions, were the daughters of Mr. Lee who had been first in the law profession, but afterwards embraced the stage as his calling. This was, no doubt, of influence on the two daughters; for both wrote some dramatic pieces. In 1784 the elder published *The Recess, or a Tale of other Times.* The subject is taken from the time of Queen Elizabeth, and this work is one of the earliest English historical romances. In 1799 Harriet Lee published the first volume of the *Canterbury Tales* which she and her elder sister afterwards extended to five volumes. The chief part is due to the younger sister Harriet; the elder sister Sophia wrote only two tales: *The Young Lady's Tale* and *The Clergyman's Tale.* The plan of the Misses' Lee *Canterbury Tales* is the same as that of Chaucer's famous *Canterbury Tales:* A company of seven persons are travelling, and in order to drive away the tediousness of time each one relates a story.

The works of Harriet Lee are considered "as standing upon the verge of the very first rank of excellence; that is to say, as inferior to no English novels whatever, excepting those of Fielding, Sterne, Smollett, Richardson, Defoe, Radcliffe, Godwin, Edgeworth and the author of Waverley"[36]). [I have quoted this passage on purpose in order to put together the great names of the English novelists until the time of Thackeray, Dickens, and Bulwer Lytton.]

William Godwin, son of a dissenting minister, was born in 1756 in the county of Cambridge. Educated at a dissenting college, he became a dissenting minister at a village; but his ambition not finding sufficient food in this humble sphere of life, he abandoned the chapel, went to London and applied himself wholly to literature. His mind was of a revolutionary turn; he recognised no authority. In 1793 when the minds of the people were stirred up by the French revolution, he published his *Enquiry concerning political Justice and its influence on General Virtue and Happiness.* In this work he develops his revolutionary ideas: He rejects marriage as a system of fraud, as the worst of monopolies; he advocates the division of capital, and the education of the young in public nurseries. However, it must be stated that

---

[36]) vide Blackwood's Magazine's vol XII. (Chambers's Cyclopaedia of English Literature 156.)

although these were his principles, he shuddered at the thought of their being put by the mob into practice[37]). In 1794 he published his novel *Things as they are, or the Adventures of Caleb Williams*. Besides some more political, ultra-liberal, and moral essays he wrote four more novels: *St. Leon, a tale of the XVI. Century 1799* — the hero resolves the great problem of the alchemists to change metals into gold and to renew youth — *Fleetwood* 1804, *Maudeville* 1817, *Cloudesley* 1830 which last three novels are of no value. Notwithstanding his numerous literary productions his circumstances were very penurious. . He died in London 1836 aged eighty years. The work on which his fame reposes, is Caleb Williams, to which our further remarks shall be confined. The author himself had a very high opinion of the moral influence of his work; for he says himself: "I will write a tale, that shall constitute an epoch in the mind of the reader, that no one, after he has read it, shall ever be exactly the same man that he was before"[38]). This novel is an autobiographical tale written by its hero Caleb Williams whose life was a "theatre of calamity"[39]). The other characters are Mr. Falkland, a refined English gentleman of literary tastes and chivalrous habits whose God — I may say — is his honour[40]), and Barnabas Tyrrel, a true model of an English country-squire, unlearned in science but well versed in "the science of horseflesh and eminently expert in the arts of shooting, fishing and hunting." The descriptions of both Falkland and Tyrrel are masterly drawn. Between these two gentlemen there existed a rivalry who should have the greatest influence in the county. Falkland who had often tried in vain to make friendship with his rival, one day when he was greatly provoked by him, murdered him in a fit of passion. Falkland being accused of the crime is acquitted by the jury, and afterwards, a former tenant of Tyrrel, Hawkins, and his son were charged with the murder of Tyrrel, and being found guilty they underwent the penalty of death. Falkland who had suffered the Hawkinses to be hung, had since the time of the murder or rather triple murder no moment of repose. Caleb Williams who entered his service as

---

[37]) cf. Biog. Notice in Lond. Gent. Mag. June 1836, 666—670. (Allibone's Dict. 684.)

[38]) vide Preface written by Godwin to Caleb Williams.

[39]) vide Caleb Williams by Godwin. chapt I.

[40]) cf. Hazlitt's Spirit of the Age. (Allibone's Dict. 684.)

a secretary, spied in the cause of his melancholy and discovered the awful truth. Falkland made him swear by a most sacred oath to keep the secret, till, at last, Caleb Williams indicted the murderer to the tribunal, and Falkland himself avowed the crime. The whole tale may be expressed in these few words: A man of a noble nature, jealous of his reputation, has committed one crime which he tries to conceal.

The book like-the other writings of the author refers to the injustice of human institutions and turns against the establishments of human. society. His language is often very impetuous: e. g. "Honour, justice, virtue are all the juggle of knaves! If it were in my power, I would instantly crush the whole system into nothing[41]!" I still refer to that passage in which the author expresses the proud national feeling of an Englishman: "I am an Englishman, and it is the privilege of an Englishman to be sole judge and master of his own actions"[42].

Part Second.

Chapter IV.

In the preceding chapters I have already spoken of several authoresses of novels; I now have to say that a very great number of novelists in England are to be found among the ladies. They show even more aptness in picturing the common life than most men do. Their observations are more minute and their way of telling stories is more delicate. In novels written by men there are often passages which offend a tender, moral feeling, but ladies even avoid being equivocal. No doubt they are often too sentimental making up whole volumes of love-tales *(Neva's three Lovers* by Mrs. Harriet Lewis[41]); *A Wonderful Woman* by Mrs.

[41] vide Caleb Williams by Godwin.
[42] cf. 'Civis Romanus sum' what the ancient Romans used to say.
[43] vide The London Journal Nr. 1407—1430.

Agnes Fleming, Chapter IV being headed *Love under the Lamps,* Chapter VI *Asking in marriage,* Chapter X *Before the Wedding*[44]). Ladies have a natural talent for exhibiting the lively, conversational parts. The chitchat we read in novels written by them, is a true reproduction of life's every day talk[45]). — I, therefore, regarded it always as very useful for those who wish to get introduced into familiar conversation to read such — I may call them — conversational novels.

As representants of that large class of female writers, Miss Maria Edgeworth, Miss Austen, Charlotte Bronte, and George Eliot deserve particular attention. The former two authoresses whose literary career falls in the beginning of this century will be treated in this chapter; the latter two of whom the one died only some years ago and the other is still penning works wich attract general attention will be spoken of in a later chapter.

The first female novelist is undoubtedly Miss **Maria Edgeworth.** She was born about 1765 in Oxfordshire; at the age of twelve, she went over to Ireland where she spent the greater part of her life, living at the country-seat Edgeworthtown, county of Longford. She first appeared as an authoress in 1801 by publishing an essay on *Irish Bulls* which she wrote in partnership with her father Richard Lovell Edgeworth, an Irish gentleman who was much addicted to literature and directed the education of his talented daughter. She has written during her long literary career for the old and the young; she accomplished the latter task with a perfection never equalled. Her educational series is known under the name of *Early Lessons* containing the tales *Frank, Rosamond, Harriet and Lucy, The grateful Negro, Little Dog Trusty* etc. Those tales are written with the greatest simplicity, so that every child may be able to understand them. They relate events of our childhood with the purpose of imparting some moral truth. I shall give a short outline of one of these tales: *Little Dog Trusty*[46]), — There were two little brothers, Frank and Robert; the former always told the truth, the latter always told lies. One day whilst they were playing, they broke a basin of milk. Frank, the truthful boy went to tell it his parents, but Robert, from fear of the

---

[44]) vide The London Journal No. 1430 et seq.

[45]) cf. Edinburgh Review 1830. (Chambers's Cycl. of Engl. Lit. 452.)

[46]) vide Dr. Peters' Englisches Lesebuch. 26.

punishment, told his mother the little dog which happened to be in the room had thrown it down. His mother was just about to give a beating to the little dog when Frank came crying as loud as he could: "Stop! Stop! dear mother, the little dog did not do it!" At the same time his father came home who hearing what had happened whipped his son Robert because he was a liar, and gave the dog to Frank as reward because he was a boy of truth. Any one may take up Miss Edgeworth's *Early Lessons,* and he will feel himself convinced of the simplicity and truth of these charming, nice tales which have such a great effect on the mind of children. In 1804 Miss Edgeworth published the *Popular Tales* which were followed in 1809—1812 by the *Tales of Fashionable Life,* the former illustrate the life and manners, virtues and foibles of the middle classes, the latter of the aristocratic class. In those tales most of her characters are Irish, and she has done for Ireland what Sir Walter Scott afterwards has done for Scotland. Scott himself says he had been induced by "the extented and well merited fame of Miss Edgeworth whose Irish characters have made the English familiar with the character of their gay and kind-hearted neighbours of Ireland, to attempt something of the same kind for his own country, without being presumptuous as to hope to emulate the rich humour, pathetic tenderness, and admirable tact which pervade the works of his accomplished friend"[47]). A better and weightier praise could not be given to Miss Maria Edgeworth than those words of Walter Scott, that great magician of Romance-writing, whose preceptress, we truly may say, she has been. It is interesting to notice that Miss Edgeworth paid a visit to her disciple in describing local characters and manners, Sir Walter Scott, at Abbotsford in 1823 and that the latter returned her visit two years later by going over to Ireland to see her at her own home at Edgeworthtown[48]). Never two greater novelists met together. In Miss Edgeworth's writings there is no enthusiasm; a sound, practical[49]) view of the duties of life pervades her books, admonishing men to look carefully after their affairs and to rely on their own exertion, to keep out of debt and not to spend more than their earnings. However, she does not consider life as a mere

---

[47]) vide General Preface (1829) to the Waverley Novels by Sir Walter Scott.
[48]) vide Chambers' Cycl. of Engl. Literature. 463.
[49]) vide ibidem 464:
        'She was a strict utilitarian.'

matter of pounds, shillings, and pence (as the English say) because wealth alone cannot secure happiness. I cannot help mentioning one or two of this authoress' *Popular Tales* which are most striking on account of their practical usefulness. *To-morrow* [50]: this is a biographical sketch of a man of great talents, but who could not get on because he put off everything to the last moment when it was too late. This biography is an illustration of the proverb: Never put off until to morrow what can be done to-day. *Rosanna* [51]) is a tale of Irish life and manners. Two opposite characters are represented in it; both are contented with their present situation: the one submitting to evils without striving to remedy them, is an indolent man; the other struggling with adversities to overcome them, is an energetic man. From among Edgeworth's *Tales of fashionable life* I shall select Vivian. There is a great deal of politics in this novel so as to surprise one that a lady has written it. It reminds one of the novels of one of our contemporaries: B. Disraeli. The party-politics are fully explained. The true patriot whose aim is the good of his country, is opposed to the vile politician whose only object is to get into power and good places. The hero Mr. Vivian is a weak man who is easily duped and led to profligacy by the intrigues of his false friend, Mr. Wharton. Afterwards he devotes himself to politics at first as a true patriot, but then abandoning the path of public virtue and integrity against his own better knowledge. "To see the best, and yet the worse pursue" [52]) that is our hero's character. His tutor and friend the Rev. Russel is a real paragon of friendship and disinterestedness, virtue and self-command. Mr. Wharton who represents the profligacy of the higher classes violates the most sacred duties as a husband and friend. Miss Bateman is one of those literary ladies of England who profess free moral principles and strive to make woman independent. The minor characters, the vain Lord Glistonbury, the affectionate but wordly Lady Vivian, the gentle and self-sacrificing Miss Selina Sidney are ably drawn. I still call the attention to this authoress' *Moral Tales*. She adopted this title instead af the name of novels because the novels, with some exceptions, were at a very low standard: "so much

---

[50]) vide Popular Tales by Maria Edgeworth, London: Milner and Sowerby. 301.

[51]) vide ibidem 139.

[52]) vide Vivian by M. Edgeworth: motto to ch. I.

folly, error and vice," she says, "are disseminated in books classed under this denomination, that it is hoped the wish to assume another title will be attributed to feelings that are laudable, and not fastidious" [53]).

Miss Edgeworth's last work appeared in 1834, *Helen*, a novel in three volumes whose object is to show the unhappiness caused by deceit and folly. Miss Edgeworth died in 1849 deeply lamented by all her countrymen whose bodily and moral welfare she had striven to improve. Before leaving this lady's writings I remark that, in my opinion, her books are well adapted for being read in schools: *Early Lessons (The grateful Negro, Little Dog Trusty, Frank, Harriet & Lucy)* for junior pupils, and the *Popular Tales* for senior pupils.

The next great female novelist is **Miss Austen.** She was born in 1775 at Steventon in Hampshire where her father was rector. After Mr. Austen's death who had directed the education of his daughter, the family removed to Southampton and thence to the village of Chawton where Miss Jane Austen published her four novels anonymously: *Sense and Sensibility, Pride and Prejudice, Mansfield Park, Emma.* She died at Winchester in 1817 at the early age of forty-two years. Her style is perhaps one of the most natural of all novelists. Her characters act and speak as they do in real life. The dialogue is very fluent and easy. She describes the domestic life and manners of the English country-gentlemen. I shall now speak a few more words about the authoress' *Pride and Prejudice.* Nothing simpler than the plot of this novel: it contains the history of four courtships with a description of the common familiar scenes as happen among country-families. There are no startling events except perhaps the one of the elopement of Mr. Wickham with Mary Bennet, no crimes, no murder; this novel resembles the smooth surface of a mirror in which the character of each person is reflected. Let us now display the rich variety of characters of this novel. Mr. Bennet is a quiet country-gentleman, not without interest for literature, for the authoress says of him "with a book he was regardless of time," Mrs. Bennet; a talkative woman, whose only business in life is "to get her daughters married." Miss Jane Bennet is a pretty, good-natured girl who does not speak ill of anybody and only

---

[53]) vide Advertisement to Moral Tales by Miss Maria Edgeworth.

takes the good of other people's character; "she is all loveliness and goodness! her understanding excellent, her mind improved, and her manners captivating." Her sister, Miss Elizabeth, is a clever girl; she may be called a virtue with intellect. Miss Mary is a literary lady, she reads great books, makes extracts and speaks of philosophy and psychologie. When her sisters talk of their pastimes, she gravely replies: "Far be it from me, my dear sisters, to depreciate such pleasures! they would doubtless be congenial with the generality of female minds. But I confess they would have no charms for me. I should infinitely prefer a book." Lydia and Kitty, the two youngest daughters of Mr. Bennet, are two fast, "vain, ignorant, idle, and absolutely uncontrolled" young girls who think of nothing but flirting and dancing, especially with officers. Lydia, in the course of the history, whilst spending the season at Brighton, elopes with a young officer. Mr. Bingley is rich, young, good-humoured, and lively, whereas his friend Mr. Darcy is rather proud and haughty. Mr. Hurst "lives only to eat, and drink, and play at cards." Mr. Colling is a representative of the High-Church clergy, his highest standard being the "decorum." He is, however, no sensible man. Mr. Wickham is a dissolute, unprincipled, young man who blackens another gentleman's character, elopes with a young girl under the promise of marriage without having the real intention of doing so. Such is the rich catalogue of characters introduced by Miss Austen in *Pride and Prejudice*. This authoress' novels will be found very profitable for the student of English literature, and I may recommend them to any lady or gentleman who wishes to get introduced into English conversation. The books are blameless and give us a pure and innocent pleasure[54]. Sir Walter Scott esteemed them very much, and he even read Miss Austen's very finely writen novel of *Pride and Prejudice* three times[55]. "What a pity," said he, in his Private Diary, "such a gifted creature died so early."

---

[54] cf. Archbishop Whateley: Quarterly Review. 1821. (Allibone's Dict. of Authors.)

[55] cf. Sir Walter Scott's Diary. (Chambers' Cycl. of Engl. Lit. II. 466.)

Chapter V.

At the head of the novelists of the present century we must undoubtedly place Sir **Walter Scott**. He was born 1771 at Edinburgh. His family descended from the ancient Scottish border chiefs whose deeds he celebrated in poetry and prose. As child he was of a delicate health and moreover afflicted with a lameness on one of his feet. He, therefore, spent some time with his grandfather in the country where the neighbouring ruins, the beautiful landscape, the tales and songs of the peasants made a strong effect on his juvenile mind. He was educated at the Edinburgh High School and entered the University of Edinburgh where he made only moderate progress and, from his deficiency in the Greek language, got the nickname of Greek Blockhead. After leaving the University he embraced the profession of law and was called to the bar 1792. Three years afterwards he was appointed as one of the Curators of the Advocates' Library. This office supplied him with ample means to study the ancient Scotch poetry. He travelled much in the Highlands where he collected the legends and ballads of the ancient Scottish chiefs. In 1805 he published his first chief poetical work *The Lay of the last Minstrel,* in 1808 *Marmion,* in 1810 *The Lady of the Lake.* These legendary poems secured him a high place among the poets of the age. In the year 1805 "Scott threw together" [56]) about one third of the historical novel *Waverley.* On the advice of a friend having put it aside, he, however, finished it after a lapse of eight years and published it in 1814 anonymously, fearing to risk the loss of the fame he had already obtained as a poet by his attempt of writing in quite a new style. The success exceeded his best expectations; the book was most eagerly read. From that time until 1831 he wrote that most splendid series of novels, which are the charm and delight of all readers. These novels appeared anonymously and it was only after the failure of Mr. James Ballantyne [57]), who printed them, that Walter Scott owned himself as the author of these master-works in prose fiction. In 1820 Scott was created a

---

[56]) General Preface to Scott's Waverley Novels.
[57]) Concerning Ballantyne's bankruptcy and the author's great losses and adversity, see Scott's Diary of 1826. (Allibone's Dictionary of Authors 1968.)

baronet. In 1831 his health failing he made a journey to Italy, stayed at Naples, visited Rome and Venice. The next year he returned to Abbotsford in Scotland, his beloved home, where he died on the 21st of September 1832.

I shall now speak about the *Waverley* novels; they are twenty-nine in number, twelve of which refer to private life and seventeen, to history (seven to Scotch history, seven to English history, and three to Continental history). I cannot help thinking of the pleasure which the reading of those unequalled works of prose fiction gave me. In the following I shall transcribe — with some alterations — part of a letter which, under the first impression of the reading of Walter Scott's novels, I wrote to an English gentleman.

Ryde, Mai 19th 1867 [58]).

I have read the first three volumes in a time of three weeks, viz.: The Waverley, Guy Mannering, The Antiquary. The perusal of Waverley gave me a great deal of pleasure and instruction. The plot is interesting, and the interest is still heightened by its having a historical ground. I got a good idea of the Jacobite rising in the year 1745 under the "bonnie Charlie"; the characters of several historical persons were made known to me: the Young Pretender who, by his amiable manners, won every one's heart, a prince, as Waverley, the hero of the novel, expressed himself, under whom to live and to die; Gardiner whose lamentable fate in the battle of Prestonpans spread an early gloom over this unsuccesful rising. The description of the Highland manners is picturesque; you see the chieftains rule in full sovereignty over their clansmen, and finally, after the unhappy attempt of setting a Stuart on the throne of England, their patriarchal power broken down. Good sketches are given of the balls and fetes during the sojourn of Charles at Edinburgh and Holyrood Palace. It was at first interesting for me to decipher the Scotch Lowland dialect, but at last I got tired of it, and I cannot understand — I do not speak of Walter Scott because he wishes to give his diction a Scotch air by introducing the Scotch dialect — why so many English novelists commonly use slang in their works. I cannot think it is to the advantage of the English language. You may answer these novelists do not form our standard literature. You are right; but these are the books which are most read. I may ask you: Are not Charles Dickens' works much read? I think they are, and yet we find so much slang in them as forms like "ain't &c." So I have come to speak about Charles Dickens [59])

---

[58]) This letter which I wrote almost seven years ago, may be regarded as the nucleus of this essay. April 17th 1874.

[59]) 'The mention of the Waverley Novels and their broad Scottish dialect, leads unavoidably to the remark, that, unlike the author of these matchless productions (Sir Walter Scott), Mr. Dickens makes his low characters almost always vulgar.' E. P. Whipple: N. A. mer. Rev., LXIX. 392—393, Oct. 1849. (Allibone's Dict. of Authors 500.)

without mentioning anything about the two other novels of Scott. I add only that Scott has read and studied a great deal, for he exhibits the completest knowledge of the most different branches. My astonishment was greatest about his learning of classics or rather latin literature; there is no author whom he does not quote occasionally and always suo loco. He manages it to indroduce some character in each of these novels who boasts of his classical knowledge: in *Waverley*, Bradlaugh is the scape-goat; in *Guy Mannering*, a rather funny school-master, and in *The Antiquary*, the Antiquary himself.

(The remarks I have interspersed in this letter fore-shadow the popular character of Charles Dickens' works.) Let us go on to say some more about Scott's other novels.

Old Mortality was published in 1816. It relates the struggles of the Covenanters for their religious and political liberties against the last Stuarts. The tale opens in the year 1679 and goes down as far as the reign of William III. The gloomy, stern Covenanters are opposed to the frivolous, but splendid and brave cavaliers of the royal party. The customs and belief of the Covenanters are explained. They observed a judaical observance of the Sabbath-day, declared all recreations and pastimes, as diabolical, rejected the custom of promiscuous dancing. They always used "thou" and intermingled their speech with names and quotations from the Bible, calling their enemies "sinners, Amalekites, gentiles." Among those Covenanters there was a peculiar religious sect called the Cameronians noted for their austerity and devotion. Old Mortality, a member of this sect, overexcited by his false, religious enthusiasm, even neglected his own offspring, abandoning his wife and five children whilst he himself was working, without reward, at the monuments of the Cameronians on the churchyards of Low-Scotland for upwards of forty years. I still remind of that touching and pathetic opening passage [60]) in which Scott describes the joyous burst of the children after the school-hours are over, and the dull, solitary, and painful duties of the school-master. Such descriptions show Scott as great in depicting scenes of quiet, private life as he is the unequalled master of reproducing departed historical epochs, characters and manners.

The Bride of Lammermoor published in 1819 is the most gloomy and melancholy of Scott's tales. It is founded on the annals of an ancient Scotch family. Fatalism which urges man on to perdition, is the principal idea of this sad tale. Lady Ashton

---

[60]) vide Old Mortality ch. I.

has pledged her faith to the master of Ravenswood; but her parents not approving of her choice compelled her, even advocating a passage out of Scripture, to reject her betrothed and marry another richer suitor, Bucklaw. The marriage ceremony took place, and on the evening whilst all the guests were dancing, a shrill yell was heard. The parents of the bride rushed to the bridal room, and on opening the door, they found the body of the bridegroom lying on the floor flooded in blood and the bride herself couching in the corner of the chimney, her night clothes torn and dabbed with blood. The bridegroom recovered, but the bride died in a delirious fit. Her lover, the master of Ravenswood, likewise met a fatal end, perishing in the depths of the quicksands whilst riding to a duel to encounter the brother of his lamented betrothed. *The Bride of Lammermoor* is Scott's Macbeth; it reminds one of the tragedies of ancient Greece.

Ivanhoe, the favourite novel of Walter Scott's writings, was published in 1820. It describes the chivalrous period of Richard Lion-Heart. Tournaments, lists, banquets are represented in the most dazzling pomp. The rough, oppressed, honest Saxon "who knows how to keep his word, even when it has been passed to a Norman," is opposed to the noble, chivalrous, victorious Norman. The marriage of the Norman Wilfred of Ivanhoe with Rowena, daughter of the Saxon Cednic is the emblem of the future union of the two races which now make up the English nation. Robin Hood, the outlawed forester, and the jolly friar are masterly drawn. Scott as always wishing to help the sufferers, awakens our sympathy with that nation which, at that time, was so cruelly persecuted, the Jews. Rebecca, the Jewess, is Scott's finest female character, full of gentleness, gratitude, and self-sacrifice. Time and space will not allow me to enter into further details of Scott's novels, I shall only be able to glance at them.

The Monastery and *Abbot* (1820) delineate the character of that most charming and unhappy queen, Mary of Scots. *Kenilworth* reproduces, with all its splendour, the time of Queen Elizabeth. The finale catastrophe of *Kenilworth* reminds us of the author's painful tale *The Bride of Lammermoor. The Pirate* contains two fine female characters, the sisters Minna und Brenda. *The Fortunes of Nigel* illustrate the reign of James I of England, "the greatest fool of christendom." *In Quentin Durward* the sly, unscrupulous, superstitious Louis XI of France is opposed to the

brave, openhearted Charles the Bold of Burgundy. *The Talisman*
refers to the third crusade: the christian king Richard Lion-Heart
and the mahomedan sultan Saladin rival in bravery and magna-
nimity. In *Woodstock* the author describes the time of Cromwell,
the victorious general of the infant Commonwealth, the master of
his soldiers' hearts whose sword swayed England. The voluptuous
character of Charles II is strongly drawn by his love-making to
Alice Lee, daughter of the faithful cavalier Sir Henry Lee, under
whose roof he had found a shelter, in the disguise of a page. The
struggle between the Presbyterian minister and the Independent
minister is truly dramatic. Scott's last novels, *Count Robert of
Paris* and *Castle Dangerous,* appeared the year before his death.
They clearly show the gradual decline of the author's genius.
Scott's greatness reposes on his reproducing departed ages and
characters and describing the manners, customs, and scenery of
his native country[61]). He is the first novelist of all ages and
nations[62]). His works are free from immoral filthiness and cor-
ruption; they are highly moral without assuming a didactic tone.
The Waverley novels have been translated into most European
languages; however, I think, a foreigner who is not somewhat
acquainted with English and Scotch history, and the religious life
of the various sects which have sprung up in England, will scarcely
be able to understand those of Scott's works that refer to English
or Scotch history. In his private life, Scott was most affable.
Isaac Disraeli speaks of him in the following terms[63]): "The finest
genius of our times (i. c. Sir Walter Scott), is also the most
delightful man; he is that rarest among the rare of human beings,
whom to have known is nearly to adore, whom to have seen to
have heard, form an era in our life; whom youth remembers with
enthusiasm, and whose presence the men and women of the world
feel like a dream from which they would not awaken. His
bonhomie attaches our hearts to him by its simplicity, his
legendary conversation makes us, for a moment, poets like
himself."

---

[61]) cf. W. H. Prescott: Biog. and Crit. Miscellanies. (Allibone's Dict. of
Auth. 1976.)

[62]) 'Sir Walter Scott is universally considered as the greatest novelist of
imagination of this century' — Sir Archibald Alison: Hist. of Europe, 1815—1852,
chap. V. (Allibone's Dict. of Authors 1977.)

[63]) vide Miscellanies of Literature by J. Disraeli. Literary Character.

Walter Scott as a novelist had many imitators amongst whom I only mention James and Ainsworth.

George Payne Rainsford James (1801—1860) is one of the most prolific writers of the age. He has written a great many historial tales, his works amounting to the number of one hundred and eighty-nine volumes. He is especiallyversed in French history. *Richelieu*, published 1829, is considered to be his best historical romance. In 1832 he issued a *History of Charlemagne,* in 1837 *Attila.*

William Harrison Ainsworth, born 1805 at Manchester, is the author of several historical novels illustrating epochs of English history. *The Tower of London* contains the history of the short reign of Lady Jane Gray, surnamed the Twelfth-day Queen, who entered the Tower of London as Queen on the 10th of July 1553, was deposed by order of the council nine days after, imprisoned in the Tower by Queen Mary, and beheaded in the year 1554 on the 12th of February, on the charge of high-treason. This novel gives a minute description, with all historical recollections, of that most ancient Tower of London of which every part, every spot recalls to Englishmen some great event of national history. Many a man had been imprisoned in its walls, many a righteous and liberal man had been tormented within its inclosures for his religious or political opinions, many a nobleman, nay even three queens had been beheaded within its precincts. The author succeeds to interest for the plot of the story; we follow the destiny of Jane Gray and her husband Lord Guilford Dudley with suspense until that fatal hour when "the fairest and wisest head that ever sat on human shoulders fell" under the axe of the headsman. The most varied events are introduced by the author: meetings of parliament, riots, sieges, pageants, duels, burning of heretics, love-scenes. The whole book is one which will be read with interest. Among Ainsworth's other novels I mention *Guy Fawkes, Windsor Castle, The Star Chamber* — all names familiar to the student of English history. James and Ainsworth excel in narrating events; their works are a rich fountain of historical knowledge.

Chapter VI.

Among the innumerable novelists of our own days there are three great names which stand out with distinction: Bulwer Lytton, Dickens, Thackeray.

Sir Edward Bulwer Lytton born 1805 was the son of General Bulwer. His mother whose maiden name was Lytton — hence the novelist's surname Lytton, — was a highly educated woman to whom the author owed much. "From your graceful and accomplished taste," says Bulwer Lytton, "I early learned that affection for literature which has ·exercised so large an influence over the pursuits of my life; and you who were my first guide, were my earliest critic [64]." Already in the year 1820 at the age of fifteen years he published a printed book *Ismael, an Oriental Tale, with other poems, written between the age of thirteen and fifteen.* Bulwer studied at Cambridge and, during the holidays, he travelled over England, Scotland, and France. His first literary productions were poetry; he had, however, no natural poetical genius. He attempted almost every kind of composition: he wrote poetry, dramas (the well known *Lady of Lions*), political and philosophical essays, and novels. In the following I shall only speak of him as a novelist. His first novel, *Falkland,* appeared in 1827, and, in the following year, he published *Pelham or the Adventures of a Gentleman.* The same year he issued *The Disowned.* These novels are wanting true morality, describing the light and easy manners of the beginning of the nineteenth century. *In Derereux* published 1829 the author sketches the time of Bolingbroke, that crafty English statesman who flourished in the latter part of the reign of Queen Anne. The scene is partly in England, partly in France, Russia, and Italy. This novel gives a wide range to the author's vast knowledge of history, politics, and philosophy. Many historical persons are introduced: Louis XIV, Madame de Maintenon, the Duke of Orleans, James III. of England, the Old Pretender, Peter the Great, Richard Cromwell. The hero of this novel, Devereux Morton, has good, moral principles. His unhappy love to Isora in which he has his own brother Aubrey as a rival, is the leading theme of the story. The catastrophe is awful. Aubrey murders Isora, the bride of his brother Morton, on her wedding-night. In 1830 Bulwer issued *Paul Clifford* and the next year *Eugen Aram.* In the winter of 1832—33 whilst staying at Naples he wrote nearly the whole of the novel entitled *The last Days of Pompeii.* This romantic fiction illustrates the

---

[64]) vide Bulwer's Dedication to his Mother prefixed to the first collected edition of his works in 1840.

grand catastrophe of the eruption of the Vesuvius in the year
79 A. D. which destroyed Pompeii. It was no doubt an arduous task
for a modern writer to reproduce the ancient world in such a
work whose chief aim ought to be to copy life as it is. In reading
Pompeii I was rather disappointed; for it does not breathe that
spirit of antiquity which we are accustomed to from the writings
of Cicero, Caesar, Livy, and Tacitus. We must, however, well
remember in order not to undervalue the novelist's task that the
Romans, in common life, did certainly not speak, feel, and act as
those great writers in their lofty style represented them to do[65]).
Bulwer describes the Roman civilisation mingling with the Grecian
at Pompeii, and introduces representants of the Egyptian world.
There are also many passages referring to that new religion which
had risen in the East and had just began to spread over Italy.
The following passage resumes the common belief of the people
concerning the Christian religion. "A dread sect! It is said that
when they meet at nights they always commence their ceremonies
by the murder of a new-born babe; they profess a community of
goods too — the wretches!" People regarded the followers of the
new creed as the enemy of mankind; they were commonly called
"Atheists." The final catastrophe, the destruction of Pompeii, is
described with awful sublimity. *Rienzi*, the Last of the Tribunes,
a historical romance, was the next of Bulwer's works which he
had already begun at Rome before he commenced writing the
preceding novel; on removing to Naples "he threw it aside for *The
last Days of Pompeii,* which required more than Rienzi the advantage of residence within reach of the scenes described[66])." This
romance illustrates the struggle of Rienzi for the liberty of the
Roman people against the usurpation of the nobility. The scene
is at Rome and the time about the middle of the fourteenth century when the Popes resided at Avignon. Rienzi, like most cham-
pions for the liberties of the people, met a violent end being put
to death by that very crowd for whose weal he had been labouring.
The parting scene of Rienzi and his beloved wife Nina is most
touchingly narrated. Rienzi wished her to fly when the populace
furiously approached, and a friend of Rienzi attempting to drag

---

[65]) cf. Essays, Polit., Hist., and Miscell. Edin. and Lon., 1850, III. 538.
orig. pub. in Blackw. May, Sept. 1845. (Allibone's Dict. of Authors 1152.)
    [66]) vide Preface to the first Edition of Rienzi by Bulwer.

3*

her away, she exclaimed. "I am the wife of Cola di Rienzi, the great Senator of Rome, and by his side will I live and die[67])!" Bulwer wrote two more historical novels. *The Last of the Barons* describes the time of Warwick, the Kingmaker. I only allude to Adam, represented as the precursor of James Watt, who had sacrificed youth, health, hope, life to his great idea of making steam serviceable to man, but like many a learned man was scoffed at and held a sorcerer, and to his angelic daughter Sibyll who justly says: "As man's genius to him, is women's heart to her[68])."

Harold the Last of the Saxons relates the short struggle of the Saxons against the Norman invasion. From amongst the author's social novels I mention *Ernest Maltravers* and *My Novel or Varieties of English life*. *Zanoni* is a peculiar kind of prose fiction, I may call it an allegorical novel. In Bulwer's later novels there is a better moral feeling based on sound principles. Bulwer Lytton who also took part in politics being several times returned as member of parliament — that great ambition of all English men — was created a baron in 1838. He died on the 18th of January 1873 at the age of sixty-seven years and was buried at Westminster-Abbey, that venerable building where the great men of England find their last repose.

Charles Dickens, the great popular novelist, was born 1812 at Landport, near Portsmouth. A few years after his birth his father removed to London where our author spent the greater part of his life. He became early acquainted with the manners of the middle and low class-people of London whose peculiarities and oddities he afterwards illustrated in his most original writings. Charles Dickens, like Walter Scott, was destined to the law; he was long enough employed at an attorney's office to get a knowledge of the law proceedings in order to be able to sketch them in his later career. He, however, preferred becoming a parliamentary reporter. As such he greatly excelled, and being thus connected with the political life of his country he got such a knowledge of politics as enabled him, in his later years, as a novelist to speak about them from his own experience. Thus before appearing as a writer he accumulated those stores of practical

---

[67]) vide The Last of the Tribunes. Lon. Chapman and Hull 1858. pg. 297

[68]) vide Chamber's Cycl. of Engl. Lit. 640.

knowledge on which his fame as a novelist was to be founded.
In 1837 he began that humorous, most laughable, inimitable series
of sketches *The Pickwick Papers* which every one in England reads
over and over again [69]). They represent the adventures of a
Cockney sportsman, that is of a Londoner. They are no connected
tale but a series of adventures. Dickens ridicules everything: the
Club-life, the elections, the parliamentary life, the law-proceedings,
even the learned investigations of antiquarians. The chief hero
is that funny gentleman Samuel Pickwick G. C. M. P. C. (i. e
General Chairman Member Pickwick Club) [70]). He and his friends
meet with the most laughable and oddest adventures. What could
be droller than that he should be accused of a breach of promise
by his housekeeper, a widow [71])! Dickens published *The Pickwick
Papers* under the name of Boz; they were humorously illustrated
by an artist Mr. Hablot Browne who assumed the name of Phiz.
A few mouths after the publication of the *Pickwick Papers* Dickens
began *Nickolas Nickleby*. It contains the life of a poor merchant-
clerk who, by his own energy, rose to become first the partner,
then the sole possessor of an important business. The chief
interest of this book is derived from its treating a social evil
which existed in England, but which is now dying out. In England private schools are not under the control of Government, and
any one may set up a school. The consequence is that many
boarding-schools exist or rather existed which were solely kept by
their "managers" as a means of gain. The children were shame-
fully neglected; not only their moral and intellectual welfare was
not attended to, but also their bodily health was ruined by their
greedy school-masters. Dickens in order to convince himself of
the bad state of education went purposely on a journey to York-
shire where the worst schools were reputed to be. He, then, drew
his description of Mr. Squeers' Academy from life. The monstrous

---

[69]) cf. Lond. Quart. Review, LIX. 484; Oct. 1837. (Allibone's Dict. of
Author's 500.)

[70]) If an Englishman has got . a degree or is member of any learned
society, he puts behinds his name initials indicating his degree or membership
of such or such a society, e. g. William Russel M. A. i. e. Master of Arts;
Thomas Eagles F R C S. i. e. Fellow of the Royal College of Surgeons. Englishmen of the learned professions being very eager to affix such appendices to their
names, Dickens ridicules this mania of his countrymen by the above enigmatic
initials.

[71]) vide The Pickwick Papers by Dickens. ch. XXXIV.

picture of Mr. Squeers was not exaggerated; for many of the York-
shire schoolmasters thought themselves to be the original, even
"one worthy actually consulted authorities learned in the law, as
to his having good grounds on which to rest an action for libel[72])."
I shall transcribe the following to characterise the school-keeping
of those Yorkshire school-masters of whom Mr. Squeers is a type.
"Both Mr. and Mrs. Squeers viewed the boys in the light of their
proper and natural enemies; or in other words, they held and
considered that their business and profession was to get as much
from every boy as could be possibly screwed out of him[73])."   In
his next work *Oliver Twist* Dickens painted London's wretchedness
and misery, such as we see it still to-day at Whitechapel (the
eastern part of London), where the dwellings of the poor are
nasty, foul holes, the poor children are dirty and almost naked,
the women pale and haggard from hunger and disease, and the
men, drunkards and ruffians.   Dickens knows how to touch the
heart in describing the life of the poor and miserable; many a
tear has been shed in reading his mournful sketches.   His novels
belong to the Real School depicting life in its stern reality.   His
writings aim at calling the public attention to some social grie-
vance in order to repress it.   Thus, in *Nickolas Nickleby,* he has
done much to put down the bad Yorkshire-schools, even more
than any act of parliament or any learned discussion of a scholastic
body could have done.   In the year 1842 Charles Dickens made
a voyage over to the United States where he met the most hearty
welcome from the Americans.   As result of his observations he
published *American Notes.*   In *Barnaby Rudge* Dickens described
scenes of the Gordon's Riots and in the *Tales of two Cities,* i. e.
London and Paris, the trials and sufferings of a French refugee
at the time of the French revolution.   From his other works I
mention the tales which he annually published at Christmas: *A
Christmas Carol, The Chimes, The Cricket on the Hearth;* these
are fairy tales which are liked very much in England. Dickens'
popularity was still increased by his public lectures.   He went
over the whole country to read portions of his own works, and
I really can say that in order to get admission one must apply
early for a ticket, for crowds of people went to hear him.   I

---

[72]) vide Preface to Nicholas Nickleby by Charles Dickens.
[73]) vide Nicholas Nickleby by Dickens. Ch. VIII. 54.

cannot help adding the following characteristic, laconic speech which Dickens made at the close of a lecture:

"Ladies and Gentlemen! In all probability I shall never see your faces again, but I can assure you that yours have yielded me as much pleasure as I have you."

When at last the funeral bell tolled the death of this popular writer, and the telegrams spread the news over the whole English world: 'Charles Dickens is no more' — it was on the 9th of June 1870 — every family felt as if one of their own had gone away. He was buried at Westminster-Abbey, where a plain marble-stone indicates his tomb with the inscription:

CHARLES DICKENS

Born 1812.

Died 1870.

William Makepeace Thackeray was born at Calcutta in the year 1811. In his seventh year he was sent over to England [74]).

He was educated at the Charterhouse School of London, studied at Cambridge and then travelled many years through France, Germany and Italy with the object of becoming an artist. On returning to England after the loss of his fortune, Thackeray was obliged to devote himself to literature in order to gain his living. He contributed to several periodical papers, among others to the Comical paper *Punch,* wrote numerous tales, critics, and poems. In the year 1846 he published his first chief work *Vanity Fair,* which was followed in 1849 and '50 by *Pendennis.* In 1852 Thackeray wrote Esmond, a description of the society of the time of Queen Anne and George I, and in 1855 *Newcomes* which is considered to be his master-piece [75]). Thackeray died in London 1863.

Thackeray is a moral writer; he paints society as it is with its faults and evils, and under the mask of satire and irony he rebukes the failings of man, their injustice and hypocrisy. In order to give an idea of the sarcastic writing of Thackeray, I shall select the beginning of Chapter XXXVI of *Vanity Fair:* "How to live on nothing a year" the contents of which are as follows:

---

[74], vide Chambers' Cycl. of Engl. Lit. 650.

[75]) cf. London Quarterly Review July 1855: "This is Mr. Thackeray's master-piece, as it is undoubtedly one of the master-pieces of English fiction. if fiction is the proper term to apply to the most minute and faithful transcript of actual life which is anywhere to be found." (Allibone's Dictionary of Authors.)

None is so little observant as not to think sometimes about the
wordly affairs of his neighbours and so extremely charitable as
not to wonder how his friend James or his friend Smith can
make both ends meet. There are families who keep a carriage,
make every year a trip to the continent or some watering-place,
have one or two boys at the College, a governess for the girls,
give splendid dinners, an annual ball with supper; yet they have
no private fortune, nor has Mr. so and so a salary large enough
to defray those extravagant expenses. How is it now that they
have not long since been outlawed? Already every one of us has
drunk a glass of wine with a friend of his, wondering how the
deuce the hospitable giver paid for it. After such general remarks
the author goes on saying that scarcely one of the guests enter-
tained at Mr. and Mrs. Crawley's did not ask the above questions
concerning them. They had been living on nothing a year, i. e.
on something unknown for two or three years at Paris, Mrs.
Crawley frequenting the fashionable salons of Paris and Mr. Crawley
playing at cards, billiards. The author then gives us an exact
account of this gentleman's skilful play by which he made a considerable sum of money which composed almost the whole of his
income. However, as Mrs. Crawley observed to her husband.
"Gambling, dear, is good to help your income, but not as income
itself. Some day people may be tired of play and then where
are we?" In short Mr. and Mrs. Crawley left Paris after some
time, under the false pretext of arranging some affairs of inherit-
ance in London, without paying the innkeeper's bill nor the milli-
ner's, nor the jeweller's, leaving, behind at the hotel, some
valueless trunks as surety for their return. It would take me too
far to follow up the farther adventures of this swindling family,
suffice it to say in order to characterise Mrs. Crawley that she
had been a governess and had allured a gentleman to marry her·
She is an "intellect without virtue," whereas Amelia, the other
heroïne of the novel, who had formed a runaway-match with her
lover, is a "virtue without intellect[76])." Thackeray's *Pendennis*
may be compared with Fielding's *Tom Jones* for as this author
has described a young man of the eighteenth century, Thackeray
depicts, in his *Pendennis,* a gentleman of our age "no better nor
worse than most educated men" are. However, there is this

---

[76]) cf. History of Engl. Lit. by Smith. 492.

difference in those two writers: Fielding plainly describes the follies
and vices, and amours of his hero, whereas Thackeray, according
to the more delicate feeling of our present society, cannot show
all the foibles and vices to which the young are subject. He must
"drape his hero and give him a conventional simper [77])." The
whole book reflects the views of our own age; whenever a gentleman or lady is introduced, the author never fails to mention, how
much he or she is worth i. e. what fortune every body has e. g.
"Mr. Welbore, though perfectly dull, and taking no more part in
the conversation at dinner than the footman behind his chair, was
a respectable country gentleman of ancient family and seven
thousand a-year." The hero Arthur Pendennis is a young man
who goes through the regular English education: Eton College
and Oxford University, enters life without settled purpose, wavering
between the profession of law and that of literature. Notwithstanding all his faults and shortcomings he is a conscientious
man; he wishes to keep his word to his pledged bride, and refuses
the greatest worldly advantages when in conflict with his con-
science. Major Pendennis is a gallant gentleman of the world;
he is member of one of the fashionable clubs of London, attends
dinners and parties in high-life. His maxims are wordly. The
gentlest characters are those of Mrs. Pendennis and of Laura Bell.
The former is the ideal of a true loving mother, the latter is the
best and purest heart whose "life is always passed in making other
lives happy."

Thackeray describes his characters from within; we recognise
the leading motives of their actions. His works are sarcastic;
however they do not want that tender affection which touches our
heart. His language is pure and noble; there is a brilliancy and
fluency superior to that of any of his contemporaries; he is the
Fielding of his age: in both is the same humour, wit, and power
of language; but Fielding oftentimes uses coarse and indecent
language, yet Thackeray always avoids indecent and equivocal
expressions. "He resembles Fielding," says Charlotte Brontë, "as
an eagle does a vulture; Fielding could stoop on carrion, but
Thackeray never does [78])."

---

[77]) vide Preface to Pendennis by Thackerey.
[78]) vide Allibone's Dictionary of Authors. 2379—80.

Chapter VII.

Referring to the division of novels put at the beginning of this essay I shall mention as representant of the descriptive novels of distant countries, **James Morier** (1780—1849). He was secretary of the embassy to the court of Persia, and resided almost his whole life in the Eastern countries. He published *Journeys through Persia, Armenia, and Asia Minor;* he wrote several novels in which he depicted eastern customs with which he had become intimately acquainted, especially with those of Persia. "The object of his first work 'Hajji Baba' was, he says, the single idea of illustrating Persian manners and customs in contrast with' those of England [79])!" The hero of *Hajji Baba* is the son of a barber who passed through various vicissitudes. He married a rich widow and was sent as interpreter with an embassy to England [80]). Great is the astonishment, even bewilderment of the Persians at our European customs and institutions. In Persia people eat with their fingers, and they regarded our knives and forks as instruments of offence which were well adapted to adorn the girdles of the Shah. The representants of English society and power do not find much favour in their eyes, for they call them "swine-eating infidels, shaven, impure, walkers on foot, obscure mortals, living in regions that know not the warmth of the sun [81])." In another novel *Ayesha, the Maid of Kars,* Morier gives some splendid descriptions of Eastern countries; he introduces an English Lord who falling in love with a Turkish maiden, carries her off to Constantinople; on his journey he is captured by the Turks and sent to the galleys. After his release he returns to England with his bride who finally turns out to be the daughter of an English Lord.

From among the writers of marine novels, a kind of prose fiction essentially English, on account of England's ascendancy on the sea — I shall select Captain **Frederick Marryat** who occupies the first place in his descriptions of sea-scenes. He was born in

---

[79]) vide Chambers's Cycl. of Engl. Lit. 496.

[80]) Sir Walter Scott remarks that Hajji "may be termed the Oriental Gil Blas." (vide Allibone's Dict. of Authors.)

[81]) vide Chambers's Cycl. of Engl. Lit. 497.

1792, entered the navy at an early age and took part in several naval expeditions in which he signally distinguished himself. He wrote about thirty volumes. He died at Langham, in Norfolk, in the year 1848.

His first novel appeared in 1829: *The Naval Officer.* "This is the most seamanlike composition that has yet issued from the press. We recommend it to all who live at home at ease, and need scarcely say that no man-of-war's man should remain an hour without it [82])." The author shews an intimate acquaintance with the scenes at sea he describes. He portraits the rough sailor as well as the saucy midshipman and the prudent captain. I quote the following passage from his novel *The 'King's Own* to show his easy way of writing:

"Captain: By the by, Sir, I understood you were not sober last night? Ship's Carpenter: Please your honour, I wasn't drunk — I was only a little fresh [83])."

Many of his characters are very humorous as the story-telling Captain, and we cannot help laughing at them. In *Peter Simple* there is an excellent description of the West-Indies. This novel is considered to be his best. "Marryat would have stood in the first class of seascribes had he written nothing but *Peter Simple* [84])."

Some parts of his works are rather difficult to understand on account of the many technical marine expressions, and even our dictionaries do not help us much.

Chapter VIII.

There are still many remarkable writers as **B. Disraeli**, that great statesman, who ever will be famous by his most brilliant and dazzling novels partly political and philosophical, **Anthony Trollope** who reproduces common stories of life, **Charles Kingsley** who may be called the representant of the "School of Muscular Christianity [85])," but whose works will offend many a liberal-minded reader by their sectarianism, **Wilkie Collins** who excels by dis-

---

[82]) vide London Atlas. (Allibone's Dict. of Authors. 1222.)

[83]) vide Chambers's Cycl. of Engl. Lit. 622.

[84]) vide North. (Allibone's Dict. of Authors. 1222.)

[85]) cf. The last hundred years of Engl. Lit. by Grant. 195.

playing deeply laid plots and by treating social questions aspiring to remedy cruel abuses existing in English society — whom, however, I shall now dismiss without further notice. I only add the names of some of these authors' works: *Vivian Grey*, *The Young Duke*, *Constarini Fleming or the Psychological Romance* by B. Disraeli; *Doctor Thorne, Orley Farm* by Anthony Trollope; *Westward Ho! Two Years ago* by Charles Kingsley; *The Woman in White, Man and Wife* by Wilkie Collins. These books are well worth reading and they will, with the exception perhaps of the works of Ch. Kingsley, be liked by every one.

Chapter IX.

Finally I shall speak of two female writers whom I have already mentioned in connection with Miss Edgeworth and Miss Austen, — Charlotte Bronte and George Eliot.

Charlotte Brontë (born 1816) was the daughter of a York-shire clergyman. He was an eccentric man and educated his five daughters who showed a great mental precocity, in a very ascetic way. His daughters wishing to get an independent position took situations as governesses. Charlotte Bronte and one of her sisters went to Brussels to apply themselves to the study of the French language. After a failure in school-keeping the clergyman's daugh-ters turned to literary pursuit. Charlotte Bronte who had already written before she attained the age of fifteen, twenty-two volumes of tales, dramas, and poetry, came forward in the year 1847 with a novel *The Professor* which, however, was rejected by the publisher. Then she wrote *Jane Eyre* (pub. under her nom de plume Currer Bell) which obtained immediate success, and assured the authoress a place among the first-class novelists[86]). The story describes the sufferings and hardships which a lonely governess has to undergo, especially her relations to the gentleman, under whose roof she is living, who had fallen in love with her. The authoress' life which was an unhappy and toilsome one, is partly reflected in *Jane Eyre*. This novel was followed by *Shirley* in 1849, and

---

[86]) cf. Fraser's Magazine. "Almost all that we require in a novelist the writer has, — preception of character and knowledge of delineating it, pictu-resqueness, passion, and knowledge of life. Reality — deep, significant reality — is the characteristic of this book." (Allibone's Dict. of Authors. 250.)

her last work *Villette* was published in 1853. She married her father's curate Mr. Nicholls in 1854, and died the year after her marriage in 1855. Her novels belong to the Real School of fiction. They contain excellent descriptions of Yorkshire scenery, and it was the truth of them which first revealed the authoress' real name; for a gentleman recognised the country, where Charlotte Bronte was living, from her deseriptious: No better evidence conld be given to the truth and reality of her pictures.

As last novelist I shall mention **George Eliot.** The author has assumed a fictious name and is supposed to be a lady, the daughter of a clergyman in the North of England, born about 1820, her real name being Mary Anne Evans. She published in the year 1854 *Scenes of Clerical Life* which, however, remained unnoticed. In the year 1859 she came forward with *Adam Bede* which created immense sensation among the literary world; five editions were exhausted in a few mouths. The hero of the novel is a carpenter, a true English working man. Having got by his industry the means of keeping a wife and family, he pays his addresses to a young country-girl, and is betrothed to her. She is, however, seduced by the young heir of the squire of the village. The girl not being able to bear the shame, runs away, and in her despair murders the child. She is imprisoned, sentenced to be hanged; but at the last moment her seducer arrives bringing a reprieve: she is to be deported. The young squire feels repentance, but "there's a sort of wrong that can never be made up for [87])!" The whole story is a sad tale; it makes a deep, melancholy impression on our mind. This novel contains as it is the privilege. of novels, the most various situations of life. It opens with the description of a carpenter's shop in wich the hero of the tale and five workmen are hammering and planning. It speaks of the coming of age of the young heir, of balls, of dinners, and of religious questions too. The reader is introduced into the way of thinking and feeling of the religious sect called the Methodists who seperated from the Church of England towards the close of the last century, their founder being Wesley. They wished for a simpler mode of worshipping; "they believed in present miracles, in instantaneous conversions, in revelations by dreams and visions, they drew lots and sought for Divine guidance by opening the

---

[87]) vide Adam Bede by George Eliot: The End.

Bible at hazard; having a literal way of interpreting the Scriptures."
The real heroïne Dinah is a Methodist preaching woman, and in
Chapter II we read a sermon held by that woman, one of the
noblest female figures ever drawn whose only aim in life was to
do the will of the Lord and to do good to others; it was she
who visited the poor seduced girl when in prison, and brought her
to repentance. The preaching scene is a true representation of
that peculiar religious life as it is to be met in the chapels and
streets of England, the speaker getting excited or moved by the
spirit and the congregation sighing and groaning aloud. *The Mill
on the Floss* (1860), *Silas Marner* (1861), and *Romola* (1863) are
of the same author. The latter is a historical novel illustrating
the time of Lorenzo di Medici, Macchiavelli and Savonarola. In
her last novel *Middlemarsh* (1871), the novelist returned to the
description of English country-life. George Eliot is regarded as
the greatest of the living authors [88]), her great power consisting in
the anatomy of the heart.

Conclusion.

1. The fertility of English novelists is astonishing. The great
impulse to novel-writing was given by the unexampled success of
Walter Scott. Since the publication of Waverley 1814 there have
been published in England about 3000 novels in 7000 volumes,
and at the present day there are issued every year about 100 novels
in 200 volumes [89]).

2. In closing this review of the English Novelists we may
affirm that the novel-literature of England is superior to that of
any other country. In Germany novel-writing is less esteemed, in

---

[88]) cf. The last hundred years of Eng. Lit. by Grant III. ch. V. 214.

[89]) I take the following notes from Masson's British Novelist's and their styles:
In the year 1820 there were published 26 novels in 76 vol.

„	„	„	1830	„	„	„	101	„	„ 205 „
„	„	„	1850	„	„	„	98	„	„ 210 „
„	„	„	1856	„	„	„	88	„	„ 201 „

This table shows that from the year 1830 the average number of novels
published every year amounted to one hundred in about 200 volumes.

France the novel never took such a high standard as in England; most French novelists only aim at amusement and excitement of the readers. The better class of English novels display, in their various kinds, a minute delineation of character, of the passions and feelings of man, or afford instruction from their different branches of knowledge, historical, geographical, even classical. In more modern times, they call the public attention to great social questions in order to redress existing abuses.

3. There has been great dissension about the reading of novels: some reject them entirely, others approve them. I think to fill up an hour of leisure we cannot take up a better book than any of Goldsmith's, Walter Scott's, Edgeworth's, Austen's, Dicken's, Thackeray's, Bulwer's novels. However, in giving novels into the hands of the youth we must be very careful, for there are many, great many which are written with a pernicious tendency and are stained with indelicate details which had been better left out, and whose perusal certainly will do no good to the reader. I am sorry to be obliged to exclude even those master-works of prose fiction: Fielding's *Tom Jones* and Smollett's *Roderick Random* from the reading of the young, on account of their impurity of language. "There is still another danger to be apprehended from the reading of novels. The imagination of the young of both sexes by whom novels are generally read with the greatest avidity, is filled up with wrong ideas of life taken from eccentric tales which affect to imitate real life, but deviate beyond the bounds of possibility and consistency. False ideas of happiness, manliness and virtue are instilled into the reader's mind and his quiet and happiness may be seriously endangered." We must, therefore, feel greatly indebted to those great novelists who have provided the reading public with healthy food; and we may truly agree with Mr. Laidlaw who said to Walter Scott whilst he wrote from dictation the author's *Ivanhoe:* "I cannot help saying that you are doing an immense good, Sir Walter, by such sweet and noble tales; for the young people now will never bear to look at the vile trash of novels that used to be in the circulating libraries⁹⁰)."

---

⁹⁰) vide Chambers's Cycl. of Engl. Lit. 478.